# A Note to Parents

Your child is beginning the lifelong adventure of reading! And with the **World of Reading** program, you can be sure that he or she is receiving the encouragement needed to become a confident, independent reader. This program is specially designed to encourage your child to enjoy reading at every level by combining exciting, easy-to-read stories featuring favorite characters with colorful art that brings the magic to life.

The **World of Reading** program is divided into four levels so that children at any stage can enjoy a successful reading experience:

## Reader-in-Training
### Pre-K–Kindergarten
Picture reading and word repetition for children who are getting ready to read.

## Beginner Reader
### Pre-K–Grade 1
Simple stories and easy-to-sound-out words for children who are just learning to read.

## Junior Reader
### Kindergarten–Grade 2
Slightly longer stories and more varied sentences perfect for children who are reading with the help of a parent.

## Super Reader
### Grade 1–Grade 3
Encourages independent reading with rich story lines and wide vocabulary that's right for children who are reading on their own.

Learning to read is a once-in-a-lifetime adventure, and with **World of Reading**, the journey is just beginning!

## Disney
# MICKEY & FRIENDS
## Mickey's Birthday

By Elle D. Risco
Illustrated by the Disney Storybook Artists
and Loter, Inc.

Disney PRESS
New York

Mickey woke up
and jumped out of bed.
"Good morning, Pluto," he said,
like he did every day.

Mickey ate breakfast,
like he did every day.

He did his stretches,
like he did every day.

But today was not like
every other day.
Today was Mickey's birthday!
"What should we do today?"
Mickey asked Pluto.

Mickey looked out the window
and saw his friends.
They were walking along the path
behind his house.
I wonder what they are doing,
thought Mickey.

Mickey looked closer.

Donald was carrying cups and plates.

Daisy was carrying lemonade.

Goofy was carrying
a bunch of balloons.

Minnie was carrying a big cake.

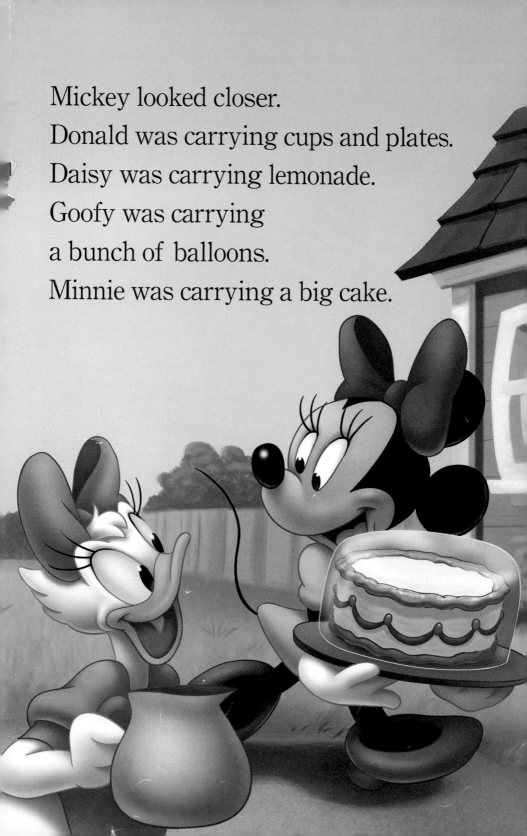

"Pluto!" Mickey said.
"It looks like they
are having a party!
Do you think it could be
a birthday party . . . for me?"

"We'd better get dressed!" he said,
"just in case!"
So Mickey dusted off his gloves
and polished his buttons.

He even brushed Pluto.
Finally, they were ready.

A little later, the doorbell rang.

Ding, dong!

Mickey opened the door.

It was Donald, and he looked upset.

"What's wrong, Donald?"

Mickey asked.

"My favorite hammock is broken,"
Donald said.
"I cannot nap without it.
Can you help me fix it?"
"Sure, Donald!" said Mickey.

So Mickey went with Donald.
As they walked, an idea
popped into Mickey's head.
Maybe Donald is <u>really</u> taking me
to my party! he thought.

Mickey was so excited that
he started to skip.

Donald stopped
near two large trees.
He looked down at the ground.
There was the broken hammock.

Mickey looked around.
There were no balloons and no cake.
There was just one friend
who needed his help.
So Mickey helped Donald
fix his hammock.

"Thanks, Mickey!" Donald said
when it was fixed.
Then Donald climbed
into the hammock and fell asleep.
"You're welcome," Mickey said,
and he started to head home.

On the way, he met Minnie and Daisy.

"Mickey!" Minnie said.

"We have something to show you!"

So Mickey went with them.

Oh boy, thought Mickey.

Are <u>they</u> taking me to my party?

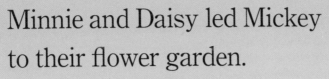

Minnie and Daisy led Mickey
to their flower garden.
"Ta-da!" said Daisy.
"Everything is blooming!"
said Minnie.

Mickey looked around.
The flowers are pretty, but
where is my party? Mickey wondered.
"Do you want to help us garden?"
Daisy asked him.
So Mickey helped water the flowers.

A few minutes later, Goofy ran up
and pulled Mickey away.
"Mickey! Mickey!" Goofy shouted,
tugging on his friend's arm.
"You have to see this!"

So Mickey went with Goofy.
Goofy seems very excited,
Mickey thought.
He <u>must</u> be taking me to my party.

"Look, Mickey!" Goofy said,
stopping by a large rock.
Mickey looked all around,
but there was no sign of a party.
Why was Goofy so excited?

Then Mickey looked down.

Two snails were racing on the rock.

"Gosh! Watch 'em go!" Goofy said.

Mickey had never seen a snail race.

It was exciting,

but not as exciting as a party.

Mickey watched for a while.
Then he and Pluto headed home.
"Oh well, Pluto," Mickey said.
"I guess I was wrong.
I guess there is no
birthday party after all."

Mickey walked up the
path to his house.
He opened his front door
and stepped inside.
As he felt for the light switch . . .

"SURPRISE!"

His friends jumped out at him.

It was a surprise party for Mickey!

For the first time all day,

Mickey had not expected it!

He was so surprised!
"I do not understand," said Mickey.
"How did you make a party
at my house?
And in secret?"

"Hyuck," Goofy laughed.
"We are pretty sneaky!"
Minnie giggled.
"We took turns
    keeping you busy," she said.

Mickey thought about his day.
Donald's broken hammock.
Daisy and Minnie's flowers.
Goofy's snail race.
Now Mickey understood.

Mickey smiled a huge smile.
"Thanks, everyone," he said,
"for the best party ever!"
His friends clapped and cheered,
"Happy birthday, Mickey!"